Party on Mars

Written by Irene Johns • Illustrated by Manu Smith

Contents

Party Plans

"I do want to have a party," said Metro.

Metro was feeling a bit grumpy. Cosmo had had his birthday party two months ago. Now Care Robot said she would have to wait for her party until their parents got back. That was three more months!

Metro and Cosmo were proud of their parents. They were Stella Science Investigators. Stella just means star, but their parents' work was important. They often had to travel in space for their work. Sometimes they were away for weeks and sometimes much longer. And that was the problem. The children were left with their very own robots, Care and Help, to look after them. Now robots can be very good at looking after children, but Care Robot and Help Robot were very strict. And it's quite hard to get a robot to change its program. Metro and Cosmo hardly ever got their robots to change their programs.

"Well," said Metro, "I am going to have a party. I'll just have to think of a way to get the Robots to change their programs!"

"How are you going to do that?" asked Cosmo.

"Well," said Metro, "I've been thinking and I'm not even going to try. Care Robot said I couldn't have my party because the Deco Robots will be in the middle of spraying new covers on all the sofas and things. Care Robot said there would be too much mess to have friends around. So..."

"I know what we could do," said Cosmo. "We could have your party at another place. But where?"

"I thought of that, too, and I know the very place. You know that new Play-in-Space Park that's just opened on Mars? That's where we'll go," said Metro.

"Wow!" said Cosmo. "That's a great idea. Let's go and ask the Robots about it."

Talking to the Robots

The rooms in the house were in a circle. The rooms were joined together with big Tube Robots. Metro and Cosmo spent a lot of time playing in the Tubes. All you had to do was stand in one end of a Tube and say kitchen or virtual-reality room or wherever you wanted to go and the Tube would spin around and take you to the right room. The children had fun trying to muddle the Tube Robots. The children would stand in different Tubes and both call out the name of the same room at the same time. It was a race to see who could get there first, but it upset the Tubes.

Care and Help didn't like Metro and Cosmo playing this game. They said it muddled the Tube Robots so much that they broke down. Then Care and Help had to mend them and they said that they had too much work to do already with two children to look after! But it was such a good game.

Metro and Cosmo went off to find Care and Help and, of course, they had to have a Tube race. They both got into separate Tubes and said kitchen, and they were off.

Cosmo got to the kitchen first. Then Metro jumped out of her Tube. Care and Help were both in the kitchen. They were nearly always there fussing over something.

"I do wish you wouldn't race in the Tubes. I've asked you not to so many times," said Help, sounding a bit cross.

"We're sorry, but it's such good fun," said Cosmo.

"Care," started Metro, "why can't I have a party?"

"You know quite well," said Care sharply. "The Deco Robots will be here for two weeks. They have to spray on new sofa covers and put new sky windows in all the roofs and a hundred other things."

"Well, if that's the only problem," said Metro, "could I have my party at another place?"

"Oh dear," said Care. "My program can't deal with this. Oh, all right, all right, you can have a party at another place. But I really don't know where we could go."

"We do," shouted Metro and Cosmo at the same time. "Mars!"

"Where?" asked Help, looking startled.

"The new Play-in-Space Park on Mars," replied Metro. "Oh, please. Please say yes."

"Well..." said Help.

"Well," said Care. "We were hoping to go there ourselves when your parents came home. They have the newest robots there. We'd like to go, too. Yes, why not? Yes, we'll all go! Now, I know it's your birthday treat, Metro, but I think you and Cosmo should both take one friend."

Metro and Cosmo jumped and shouted and danced all around the kitchen. They were so happy!

11

Asking the Friends

Everyone had a Tele Robot Pad. The Tele Robot Pads were clicked onto their arms. All you had to do was tell the Teles who you wanted to speak to and what you wanted to say and they did the rest.

"I think we should ask Juno and Jupiter to come to our party," said Cosmo.

Juno and Jupiter lived next door to each other and the four children played together every day.

"Let's send a Tele note now," said Metro. "I hope they can come on that day."

Tele notes soon beeped on Metro and Cosmo's Teles.

Yes, yes, yes please!

The Tele notes were from Juno and Jupiter. All the Tele notes said was, Yes, yes, yes please!

Journey to Mars

It was the day of the birthday party, at last. Metro's parents had sent Tele notes and pictures had flashed on Metro's Tele, too. The parents were both smiling and they had some great news. They would be coming home soon!

"What a great start to my birthday," thought Metro.

Cosmo was calling out, "Juno and Jupiter are here."

Juno and Jupiter each had a present for Metro. Juno gave Metro a black, velvety, robot spider and Jupiter gave her an even bigger dark-red glowing robot spider.

"Wow," said Metro. "I can't wait to play with them. They're too special to put with the rest of my robot spiders. I'll have to find them a special place!"

"Now, let's find the Robots and get going," said Cosmo.

He just couldn't wait to get to Mars!

The four children raced to the kitchen and, sure enough, there were Care and Help, still fussing.

"We're ready!" said Metro.

"Right, into the Tubes for the rocket ramp," said Help.

They were all in the rocket in a flash. Care spoke to Rocket Robot and told the robot where they were going. The children and Care and Help just had to sit back and relax. Metro and Juno called up the Play-in-Space Park to get the latest news and the boys talked about what they would do first.

Fun on Mars

Rocket Robot made a very smooth landing. Care and Help fussed over Metro and Cosmo and checked that they looked neat and tidy.

Metro and Juno were heading off to the giant-spider ride. Cosmo and Jupiter were going to have a good look around first, and Care and Help wanted to check out the newest robots.

"We might find a new robot to help us in the kitchen!" said Help.

"Right, children," said Care. "We'll all meet back here at the rocket in three hours. Keep checking your Teles for any notes. You mightn't hear the beeps in all this noise. You don't have to pay to go into the park, just for the things you try. Now, here are some disks. You'll need them to pay the Entrance Robots at each place and to buy something to eat. And, remember, not too many sweet things."

"Have a good time," called out Help, as Care and Help hurried off to see the latest robots.

19

Metro and Juno hurried over to the giant-spider ride. There were a lot of people already lined up, waiting. Soon it was the girls' turn.

The girls put on the padded suits and helmets and jumped on their spiders. Metro's spider was green with purple spots and a purple seat. Juno's spider was lime and orange, with a lot of stripes. The Spider Robots could do the things real spiders could do, but they had to be told what to do and then they would do the task.

"Let's make giant webs first," said Metro.

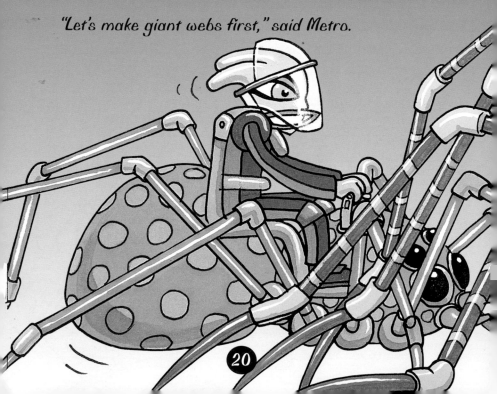

The girls found some giant twigs and the Spider Robots set to work. The webs were lovely. Metro's spider made a green-and-purple web. Juno's spider made a lime-and-orange web.

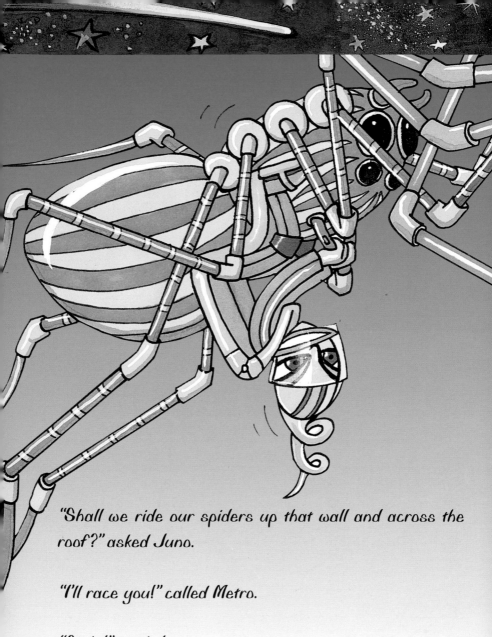

"Shall we ride our spiders up that wall and across the roof?" asked Juno.

"I'll race you!" called Metro.

"Right!" said Juno.

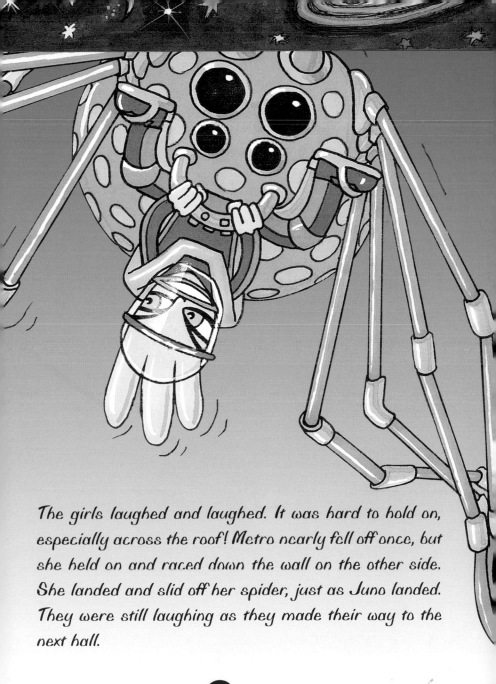

The girls laughed and laughed. It was hard to hold on, especially across the roof! Metro nearly fell off once, but she held on and raced down the wall on the other side. She landed and slid off her spider, just as Juno landed. They were still laughing as they made their way to the next hall.

Food and Fun

"Let's get something to eat," said Metro. "Look, here come Cosmo and Jupiter. We can choose some food together."

"Look at those," said Jupiter. He was pointing at some cakes called Mars Rocks. They were huge and looked like chocolate, but they were glowing! "I'm going to have one!"

"I'm going to have a Laughing Stick," said Metro. "I've been laughing so much already."

Metro bit into the creamy-yellow stick, and the stick laughed!

Jupiter and Cosmo were eyeing some shiny pink-and-silver balls and orange-and-gold nuggets that were bouncing up and down in a little tank.

"Let's try those," Cosmo said to Jupiter.

The balls came in a small clear drum. Then the fun started. Each time Jupiter or Cosmo took the lid off the drum the balls tried to jump away. Then Jupiter found a ball-size chute at the bottom of the drum. All they had to do was hold the chute over their lips and a ball jumped straight into their mouths and bounced about inside! Jupiter and Cosmo were laughing so much they could hardly eat the balls.

"We've had a great time on the Robot Spiders," said Juno. "Where did you boys go?"

"You could spend days here! First, we had a look around. Then, we went to the Mars Crater Climb. It was so cool. It looks just like a crater, but a robot climbs with you and where he points a peg pops out for you to grab. We went right to the top!" said Jupiter.

Cosmo went on, "Then, at the top, there's a huge spiral tube that goes back down to the entrance. The tube doesn't have much air pressure and you sort of float and swim to the bottom. It was great!"

"Shall we do something together now?" asked Metro.

"What shall we do?" asked Juno.

"You leave that to us," said Cosmo grinning at Jupiter. "We've had a good look around."

First, they raced on a track on hoverboards and Metro won. She was always good at sports.

Then they went to the Movie Sphere. They all sat in a floating bubble inside the sphere. The movie was all around them. It was like being inside a giant ball. The pictures, sound, and smells were spinning all around them, even under their feet! The movie was about rocket races. Jupiter wished he hadn't eaten all of his Mars Rock!

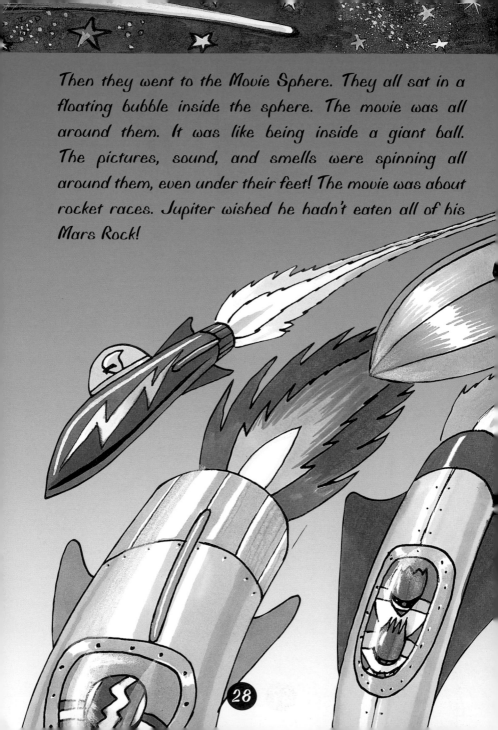

When the movie was over they still had some time left. They were wondering what to do next, when Jupiter said, "I know, follow me!"

He set off and the others had to run to catch up with him.

"Where are we going?" called Juno.

"Nearly there," called back Jupiter.

Jupiter stopped by a sign that read, Mars Bouncing.

"What is it?" asked Juno.

"Well, we each get into one of those clear Bubble Robots and tell the robot where we want to go on the side of that hill. Then you try to push the other bubbles off. If the bubbles fall off, they bounce back up again. There aren't really any rules and it's like being a part of a robot," said Cosmo.

They raced to get into their Bubble Robots. Cosmo was off first. He saw Metro coming up the side of the hill and he bounced after her. Metro was the first to get pushed off the hill, but she bounced right up again and chased after Cosmo.

Juno was the only one who didn't get pushed off the hill. She was the best driver.

Jupiter started to think again about all the Mars Rock he had eaten! But time was running out.

"Quick, come on," said Metro. "Our time's nearly up. Care and Help will be so grumpy if we're late!"

The children raced back to the rocket. They just beat the Robots back. Care and Help were looking happy, too.

"Did you all have a good time?" asked Care.

"Great!" shouted the four children together.

"Well, so did we," said Help. "And we've found such a good robot that would be a great help to us in the kitchen. We're going to speak to your mother about getting one as soon as she gets back." Help nodded happily at Metro.

"Happy birthday, Metro," they all shouted.

"Let's come back next year," said Metro happily.